HAUNTED BY
desire

Published by Valerie Lynne Books
Illustrated cover design by Concepts by Canea
Discrete cover design by Vanilla Lily Designs
Edits by Jenny Sims at Editing 4 Indies 1
Formatting by Vanilla Lily Designs

ISBN: 979-8-9895649-8-9

Chapter One

Nathaniel

"Excuse me." I grip the handle of my leather portfolio bag, tugging it beneath my shoulder. Then I shimmy around the older man stooped over his walker, slowing me down.

"Youth today," a woman, I presume to be his wife, clutches his arm, and mutters, grimacing at me. "Always rushing to get nowhere."

I pick up the pace, rushing like hell to reach the commuter bus, the one with its door wide open that I should have boarded five minutes ago. Suddenly, a toddler jumps in front of me, his mother preoccupied with the fussy baby she pushes in a stroller. "Pardon me. I've got to get to that bus before it leaves," I say as I sidestep around them.

"Yeah, whateva. You're never gonna make it," she snaps from behind me.

"And you have a lovely day too," I say under my breath.

The bus driver emerges onto the sidewalk, then stoops to remove the portable step from the ground. Adrenaline surges within me, as running is my only option.

"Hey! Watch it, asshole!" a woman dressed in business attire screams when the bag, now tossed over my shoulder, slides down my arm and bangs against hers. "You made me drop my phone."

Son of a bitch!

I turn back and snatch it for her, relieved to see it remains undamaged. "Jerk," she says, wrenching it from my proffered hand.

What the—

A sharp pain ricochets up my shin. My attention flies downward, and I'm taken aback by the set of steel-gray eyes boring into mine.

"Young man are your pants on fire?" the frail woman standing before me questions in a shaky but firm voice. Then she has the gall to poke the tip of her cane against my calf a second time, only with a softer touch than the wallop she'd given me a moment before.

I shake my head to wrap my mind around the fact that this pint-sized stranger dared to reprimand me. "Just late for work."

Her angular chin juts forward, her eyes squinting up in my direction as she assesses me. The thin lines etching the outside of her lips deepen as they curve up into a wry smile. "Do you believe in fate?"

Okay, this is ridiculous. The old lady should be thankful I don't report her to the police for assaulting me, not delaying me with stupid questions. What more does this wacko want?

"Nathaniel," she says as I walk away.

I freeze, and then slowly turn around. "How do you know my name?"

She doesn't acknowledge my question, choosing instead to spew some philosophical nonsense. "Don't waste precious time dwelling on uncontrollable things."

"How. Do. You. Know. My. Name?" I repeat the question through gritted teeth. She steps forward, shuffling toward me until she's inches away. Then she lifts a weathered hand out, placing her open palm over my heart. The touch scorches my skin, a fire erupting within me as she mumbles something incoherent.

"Get the fuck away from me!" Terrified, I'm desperate to get away, but my legs fail me. She's ensnared me in some sort of spell.

"Open your heart and your mind." Her words are louder now as her hand rolls over my pecs in a circular motion. "Don't worry, dear one. Your job will be there when you get there just as surely as you will encounter your destiny before the sun sets tonight."

I tear my gaze from hers to glance over my shoulder, noting the bus's absence. Then I whip my head back in her direction, my neck swiveling back and forth as I scan the crowded sidewalk.

She's vanished!

Chapter Two

Mia

"Don't fret, darling." I turn my attention away from the hustle of pedestrians on the sidewalk. Helen Carrington, the woman I consider my mentor, flashes what she must believe is a reassuring smile. Of course, she would say that. Chauffeured limousine rides throughout downtown are commonplace for the heiress turned successful businesswoman. Everything she touches turns to gold. However, rubbing elbows with some of Newport's most elite residents is new to me.

I play with the fidget ring that I always wear on my right hand, unable to distract myself from the possibility of upcoming doom. "What if he says no? I could say something stupid and blow it. Then what?"

Soon, I'll exit this limousine and enter *Paradise and Pleasure Magazine's* headquarters. The meeting would not be happening without Helen, whose influence made my appointment with Richard Trent, editor-in-chief, and his star reporter, Nathaniel Graves, possible.

Sunlight streams through the windows and glistens over the

diamond-encrusted *H & C* initials engraved into the compact held in Helen's palm. Sporting a pair of oversized sunglasses, she's unfazed by the blinding light as she puckers her lips before the mirror. With artful precision, she applies another layer of candy-apple-red lipstick, and I find myself in awe and wonder. What would it feel like to possess just an ounce of her confidence? Few can pull off the daring shade. Then again, no one holds a candle to Helen Carrington.

"Nonsense," she says, snapping the compact shut.

"But—"

"There will be no buts." Helen waves a manicured hand between us, bringing a halt to my negative thoughts. "Sweetheart," she says, her voice softening. "For months, you have devoted your time and energy to planning this event. You have conducted thorough research of each location and educated yourself on its haunted history."

Everything she is saying is true. Still, the intrusive, self-destructive talk creeps in. "I know. It's just that it's more than a college project or public event—it's my baby."

"I have complete faith in you." She places her hand on my arm and gives it an affectionate pat. "Now, you must believe in yourself. Don't allow self-doubt to cripple you. Stand tall and own all that you've accomplished. It's not an easy feat to be the mastermind behind such a monumental event. I couldn't be prouder of you, even if you were my daughter."

I swallow back the lump in my throat. If I believed in fairy tales, I'd say Ms. Carrington was my fairy godmother. Sometime over the past several months, she transitioned from a woman I admired from afar into a maternal figure. No words can describe my gratitude for her kindness towards me and her genuine belief that I am capable of greatness. The praise she lavishes on me regularly is overwhelming for someone whose biological mother doesn't even like her.

"Thanks," I choke out, barely able to speak. "You made this happen."

"You give me too much credit. I merely opened a few doors."

A few? She's opened dozens and given me the confidence to walk through them. And to think that, for months, I feared Helen would change her mind about helping me.

"Don't you just love people-watching?" Helen asks, tapping her fingertip against the tinted window. "Look at all those people milling about. It's a zoo out there."

I nod, knowing that she changed the subject on purpose. "I hope we get there on time. Traffic is barely moving."

"Of course we will. Sammy knows all the shortcuts."

I turn my attention back to the activity on the sidewalk. Instantly, my eyes zoom in on a hot guy speed walking through the crowd. "That's Nathaniel Graves, isn't it?"

"Scoot over. Let me see." Helen nudges my shoulder. "The one with the pink button-down?"

I nod, my pulse racing. "Yeah. He certainly looks like the same guy pictured with the rest of the editorial staff at the magazine. He is far better-looking in person. The magazine photo didn't do him justice." The pastel shirt clings to his skin, its cuffs rolled high enough to see the hint of a tattoo beneath. A dusting of dark scruff covers his determined jaw, and his no-nonsense expression give him a sexy, intelligent look.

"You have excellent taste. I can see why he captured your eye."

"Damn! That was so rude," I say, horrified as he nearly plows down a woman dressed in a business suit.

"Oh my." Helen releases a throaty laugh as we each watch him spin around and backtrack toward the woman. "By the look on her face, I can't decide whether he's brave or stupid to approach her."

"I know," I say, watching as he stoops and picks up the phone. "She needs to ease up. He's righting his wrong."

"We should all be so lucky to have that fine fella kneel before us," Helen says as the limo driver steps on the gas and picks up speed.

I bite back my response, wanting to say I'd like nothing more than to give him a thorough tongue-lashing. Instead, I pull out my notebook and study the talking points I plan to discuss, and I hope that I don't find myself so infatuated with Nathaniel Graves's looks that I can't form a complete sentence.

Chapter Three

Nathaniel

Half an hour later, I've finally arrived at *Paradise and Pleasure Magazine*. To regain my composure, I pause outside my boss's office door. My chest aches, but not from the exertion of the five-mile walk. However, I must admit that it didn't help. The freakish encounter with the witchy lunatic is to blame for its incessant thumping. It hasn't stopped since we crossed paths, and for the life of me, I have no recollection of meeting her before. It's unlikely I'd forget someone that unsettling.

I yank on the knot of my tie, smoothing it down over my shirt. My usually pressed attire is now a sweat-stained disaster, thanks to an unfamiliar maniac who gave me the heebie-jeebies. Shoulders squared, I rap on the door and step inside.

"You're late." Richard Trent is a busy man. My tardiness must have marred his morning itinerary. Richard's lips turn down as he glowers at me. "You look like shit."

"Thanks," I deadpan, lowering into one of the chairs positioned before the walnut desk. "I've had a rough start, and sadly, the day is only beginning."

"Well, you're here now. Let the attitude go, Graves."

If ... no, *when* I get the position at *Global Destinations Magazine*, I'm going to enjoy showing Richard what a real attitude looks like. I push the notion aside, eager for the details of my next assignment. After spending the previous month debunking the rumored paranormal activities reported at a run-down plantation home in Savannah, I hope to be sent somewhere in Europe. Don't get me wrong. Georgia is a lovely state, but I've reported on other sites there before. I'm ready to tackle some ancient ruins loaded with folklore. Having built a career out of exposing so-called haunted tourist attractions, I've traveled all over the world, and Europe is my favorite travel destination. Besides the satisfaction of proving to its naive occupants that they are squandering their money on a facade, I enjoy engrossing myself in old-world culture and regional cuisine.

With an obnoxious clearing of his throat, Richard opens a file folder on his desk, removing a stack of pamphlets and a stapled stack of paper. Yes, my boss is old-school. He loathes technology and prefers tangible references to a computer screen. Just one of the many reasons I wish to quit this job. Whenever he can get out of using the computer, he will. The result is a messy desk and an office that rivals any of the episodes of *Hoarders*. "As soon as Mia returns, we'll get down to business. I've a lot to discuss with both of you before my next meeting."

Both of us?

I cock an eyebrow, noting the purple paisley printed backpack lying unzipped against the leg of the vacant chair positioned beside mine. I don't recognize it as belonging to any of the other journalists, nor do I remember any of my colleagues leaving the lavender-colored spiral notebook with two purple pens tucked between its coils on the chair cushion opposite me.

"You're here!" A cheerful voice breaks the silence.

Mia, I presume.

Annoyed by her interruption, I twist around to get a look at the intruder. My heart continues to rap, but now it's for a different reason than before—a young woman with wild curly raven hair dyed with streaks of a vibrant shade of purple.

"Nature called. Of course, I had no choice but to answer." She giggles, her pretty smile warming my insides. "I saw the Keurig machine and helped myself to a cup of coffee. If you'd like, I can make one for you." I can hear her nervousness as she picks up the notebook and pens and plops down onto the cushion. "I would have gotten one for Ritchie, but he said he doesn't drink coffee."

Ritchie? Seriously?

In all the years that I've worked with Richard Trent, no one has ever referred to the tyrant as *Ritchie*. Things changed when this little ray of sunshine entered. "No, he doesn't," I say, mystified by the whirlwind dressed in solid black.

"Nathaniel Graves, I'd like you to meet Ms. Mia Sousa," Richard says.

Sousa...

This young woman bears a resemblance to a famous former supermodel and shares her last name. Her abrupt departure from a lucrative career that dubbed her the most beautiful woman in the world was tabloid fodder for months. Especially when the gossip-mongers guessed her relationship with a nerdy medical resident was behind her retirement.

"She's my sister," Mia states as if reading my mind, and then thrusts her hand out for me to shake.

I take in her Gothic attire, allowing myself the pleasure of a slow perusal from the high collar of her ruffled balloon-sleeved blouse down her hip-hugging ankle-length skirt to the black Victorian-style thick-heeled boots. "Beauty runs in the family," I say, deciding it improper to add that I prefer Mia's petite, curvaceous body to her sister's model-thin figure. Her delicate hand feels soft as it disappears within my beefy one.

A tinge of pink blushes her cheeks at my compliment. "You're very kind, Mr. Graves."

"Please call me Nate. I'm much too young to be Mr. Graves."

A hint of mischievousness dances in her huge dark eyes. "It's nice to meet you, *Nate.*"

Damn!

Even the tone in which she says my name is hot. My dick throbs as I struggle to resist the urge to bend her over the desk and have my way with her. She glances down at our entwined fingers before her attention darts back up to gift me with a wide, toothy smile. I loosen my grip, not wanting the handshake to end, but unable to tear my gaze from her. Something tells me this Gothic vixen is dangerous. I should be ashamed of myself for reacting this way toward her. She's way too young for a thirty-five-year-old man.

Richard cleared his throat once more, more aggressively than before. "Sometime today, we need to discuss your next assignment." He shoves a stack of glossy brochures in my direction. "Next Friday marks the start of Newport's first Haunted Happenings Festival."

"Sounds delightful. Lucky me, I get to write another article debunking the absurdity of the paranormal without even leaving my home state."

Mia's sparkle dims as she jolts up from her chair in opposition. "Oh, there is nothing absurd about it. Newport overflows with haunts."

"Sure, it does. Just like all the other so-called haunted locations I've debunked." I chuckle, not intending to offend her. "Believe me, Ms. Sousa, this festival will prove to be a hoax, just like all the rest."

"Nate." Richard scolds me as if I were a child. "Ms. Sousa will graduate with honors from Salve Regina University in the spring with a Master of Fine Arts in Creative Writing. She's devoted several years to gaining unwavering knowledge of the works of the macabre. Especially, the works of Edgar Allan Poe. Her consistency on the dean's list proves to me she's well-versed in her field."

"I look forward to you proving me wrong," I say.

Her plump ruby-red lips turn down into a pout, and her hands have moved to rest on her curvaceous hips as she taps her foot.

"Look, I may sound arrogant, but seriously, someone as educated as yourself can't possibly believe in ghosts. Studying paranormal folklore and how it piggybacks onto Newport's historical past is surely a stimulating pastime. Occasional escapes benefit everyone. Your literature studies will serve you well if writing stories or hosting fictitious events are your future goals."

"Not judgmental at all, are you?" She narrows her eyes. The undercurrent of challenge in their depths thrills me with the unspoken dare. "We'll see how you feel at the end of the event."

Ignoring her snarky remark, I flash my most alluring smile. "I can't wait."

"Ms. Sousa volunteers at the Newport Ladies Refurbishment Society," Richard interjects. "Lucky for us, she's agreed to be your personal tour guide for the duration of the festival."

"Oh no, no, no." I waggle my finger left and right while shaking my head. "As lovely as it is to meet you, Ms. Sousa, I don't need a host. I work alone."

Richard folds his hands atop the mess of paperwork to stare me down. The golden rule of any professional is to not mix business with pleasure. As intriguing as I find Mia, I won't jeopardize my career over a pretty face and a sexy-as-fuck body. Especially now that I'm on the cusp of obtaining the dream job that I've yearned for my entire career.

Richard looks as if he wants to wring my neck. "I understand you prefer to work alone. However, Ms. Sousa is the creator of the event and, as a result, the perfect person to provide firsthand knowledge of the festival."

Mia glowers at me, her eyes now icy dark slits. "I read your article about the Georgia plantation. It was entertaining," she says in a disgustingly sweet tone before going in for the kill. "But there is always room for improvement."

"It's nothing personal. If I needed a host, I'm sure you'd be the best I could find. But I don't." Thank God looks don't kill, or I'd be dead on the floor. "Not to toot my own horn, but I've been doing just fine on my own. If I weren't, I wouldn't be an award-winning travel journalist."

"Stop acting like an imbecile! I have the knowledge to assist you, and I'm going to do it whether you like it or not." Mia steps closer, ramming the pad of her fingertip into my chest. "Let me be frank with you, *Nate*." The emphasis on Nate is no longer sexy and sweet—it's venomous. "Being your host is a requirement for my senior project. I will not let some judgmental stick-up-his-ass idiot deter me from graduating. So suck it up, buttercup. You're stuck with me."

Damn! She's feisty. A hothead in need of taming. Hoping she doesn't notice the evidence of my attraction, I place my folded hands above the bulge of my crotch. "You know what, I like you, Ms. Sousa."

She tsks at my compliment.

Keep it up, my sexy gothic goddess, and you'll be sore for days after I spank that fine ass.

"Although I've never needed a host before, you've made an excellent case for yourself. Perhaps I'll make an exception this once." I shrug before adding, "It might be fun to have a partner in crime."

"Ms. Sousa, I like your tenacious spirit. You've met your match, Graves." Richard shoves the pamphlets back into the file folder. "As there is nothing left to discuss, my personal assistant will forward the travel itinerary to both of you mid-week. Now, if you'll excuse me, I must prepare for my next meeting. It was a pleasure to meet you, Ms. Sousa," Richard says, flashing a rare smile before turning his hard stare on me. "Goodbye, Nate."

Chapter Four

Mia

"Katie!" I bellow, kicking the apartment door shut. "Wait until you hear this!" My roommate sits in the recliner with her computer balanced on her lap, textbooks stacked at her feet, and an untouched turkey sandwich and half-full bottle of water on the coffee table.

I fling myself onto the plush sky-blue couch cushion. Dramatic? A bit, but that's me. I've always been over the top. I like it that way. Keeps everyone on their toes. Besides, what is normal anyway?

Katie's eyes grow wide as I wrench the oversized pillow from behind my back, giving it a few swift whacks, before squeezing it against my chest. If only Nathaniel Graves's neck had been there instead of a pillow.

"Things didn't go well?" Katie asks, closing the lid of her laptop.

"Um ... no! They sure as fuck did not." I swing one leg back and forth, my heel knocking against the base of the couch. In my head, I hear my mother's disapproval, scolding me for allowing my shoe to touch the furniture, which only incites my agitation more.

Brows furrowed, Katie taps her fingertips on the arm of the

chair. Best friends since high school, she's the yin to my yang. The calm to my storm. Although we both share a love of literature, our similarities end there. A die-hard romantic, Katie prefers classics such as Jane Austen or Emily Brontë. She's soft-spoken and shy, and has a passion for flowy dresses in pastel colors, while I dare to dress with artistic flair in black, violet, maroon, and indigo.

Katie knows me better than anyone else. Therefore, she remains silent. She is awaiting my full eruption.

"Nathaniel Graves is a fucking asshole! A snobbish prick!" I cross my arms over my chest. "He's going to ruin the Haunted Happenings Festival, and I'm going to end up in prison. You'll visit me, right?"

"Yes ... of course. Wait a minute—what?" Confusion etches her face. "What do you mean he ruined it? You just met him today? You hardly know him. And why am I visiting you in jail?"

"Trust me, I know enough. He's an insufferable dick. Katie, I swear to God ..." I raise my hand out before me as if I were testifying under oath. "If I spend my weekend showing Nathaniel Graves around Newport, he's going to die because I will kill him."

"Mia," Katie says, her tone much more rational than my own. "Isn't that excessive?"

"I look horrible in bright orange. It does nothing to complement my skin tone, and stripes are from the devil." I sigh. "Mother always told me to stay away from them. They make me look like an oversized egg with skinny arms and legs sticking out of a rotund body."

"Brace yourself because you won't like what I have to say." Katie bites her bottom lip. Although her tone is cautious, I can tell she's stifling her laughter. "Somehow, you must find neutral ground, or you won't pass the final project. Graduation requires you to work with him. Deal with him."

Chapter Five

Mia

I haven't been able to rid myself of the snit I've been in since I left *Paradise and Pleasure Magazine's* office on Monday. Flashbacks of Nathaniel Graves have plagued me instead of letting me devote all my energy to the festival's finishing touches. Thanks to that dipshit with his condescending tone and snide remarks, I've been second-guessing every detail of the event.

"Planning to go in sometime today?" Katie interrupts my internal rant. Seated in the driver's seat, she shoots me a pitying look while she waits for me to get out of her old, beat-up Ford, which is an upgrade from my car since it runs. My car's brakes failed at the worst possible moment, so I depend on Katie for rides. "Science isn't my forte, and we have a test today. I was hoping to make it to class a little early to review my notes."

"Sorry. I was thinking." I climb out of the passenger seat and open the back door to retrieve my backpack and the binder over-loaded with paperwork from the back seat.

"Don't worry. You've got this." Katie is the sweetest person I know. Sometimes I worry about her selflessness. Everyone knows she'd give them the shirt off her back, and I know people will take advantage if you let them. Especially her new boyfriend, Padrig. He's done nothing obvious for me to distrust him, yet something about him seems shady. I can't put my finger on it, though.

"Not worry?" I raise an eyebrow, shooting her a quizzical look. "When I have to kiss up to that jackass all weekend? Not happening."

"Maybe you both just got off to a rough start, and you'll find out he's not so bad." She shrugs.

"Katie." I release a disgruntled snort. "There is no misunderstanding. Nathaniel Graves called Haunted Happenings a hoax," I deadpan. "Are you sure you can't make it to Belcourt Castle tonight? Regardless of his actions, the food will be delicious."

"I wish I could, but Liam desperately needs my help. Delta is on maternity leave until next month. Lily is in Florida with her boyfriend, and Monica has the flu."

"Alright. I understand you have to help your brother with the family business." I'm not lying. I understand. O'Halloran's, a popular Irish pub on Lower Thames St, is always busy. It was standing room only on Friday and Saturday with people waiting to order its popular fish and chips. "If by some miracle anything changes, please come, okay?"

Katie nods as she turns the ignition. The car roars to life, drowning out her response as I slam the door. With the flash of a pretty smile, she steps onto the gas pedal, leaving me stranded on the sidewalk across from the five-story, luxurious Gilded Seashell Hotel, where the paid guests are about to convene for the first themed event.

Chapter Six

Mia

I trudge through the ornate lobby, noting Helen's frown as I approach.

"Mia, I expected you to be beaming from ear to ear, not looking as if you'd lost your best friend. Did you and Katie argue?"

"Everyone is counting on me." I step into her open arms, thankful for the comfort of Helen's embrace. "I'm not qualified. What if everyone asks for their money back?"

Kindness flickers in her eyes as she releases her hold and steps back to look at me. As usual, Helen looks flawless. Her tailor-made cornflower-blue satin suit hugs her curves, complementing her violet-hued eyes. The perfume she wears smells divine, and I can't help but wonder how long she spent straightening her thick, dark hair into the glossy, silken mass cascading down her back. "Your mother? Did she say something that bothered you?"

The question is comical, yet for once, the answer is no. Mother hadn't acknowledged the event at all when I spoke with her yesterday. "I'm just nervous."

"You have nothing to be concerned about." She pushes a tendril of hair off my cheek. "You have done everything necessary for this event to be a success. Besides, I'm your secret weapon. I won't let you fail, darling."

Relief floods through me. With those few words and her unwavering support of me, Helen has given me the boost of confidence I needed. Unable to stop myself, I throw my arms around her for another hug. "Thank you."

Heavy footsteps followed by the clearing of a man's throat echo from behind us. "It's showtime," Ms. Carrington whispers in my ear. "Don't take any shit from him, regardless of how gorgeous he is. Remember, this is your event, and you're in control," she reminds me, and steps out of the embrace. Her lips curve up into a heart-stopping smile as she proffers her hand. "You must be Nathaniel Graves."

Chapter Seven

Nathaniel

It appears the rumors are true. Helen Carrington is even more breathtaking in person than in the thousands of photographs printed in the society columns. Still, her beauty doesn't compare with that of the petite woman standing beside her. Seldom do I find myself smitten with anyone. However, Mia's aura defies words. Knowing that I'll spend the weekend with Mia as my chaperone has its benefits. It makes being forced to work with a stranger tolerable.

My lips quirk, lifting at the corners. I didn't miss Mia's eye roll. I extend my hand, wrapping my fingers around Helen's. Its warmth and satiny smoothness were in stark opposition to her firm grip. "The one and only at your service."

She arches an eyebrow, and it's obvious she didn't miss the innuendo. "It's very kind of you to offer your services, Mr. Graves. I can't speak to Mia's needs. Those you'll have to ask her yourself. However, as the founder and CEO of The Newport Ladies Refurbishment Society, I assure you, I have all the staffing I need."

Well, fuck, Graves. She told you, didn't she?

"Mia, dear," Ms. Carrington drawls. "Why didn't you tell me

that Mr. Graves was such a looker? With a handsome face such as his, I would find it hard to listen to a word this fella says." She slides her hand from mine and winks before spinning around on her sky-high heels. "Good luck with that," she adds before drawing Mia into her arms and whispering something inaudible against her ear.

Mia nods in response, and with a flip of her hand, Helen says, "Ta ta."

"Don't get your hopes up. She's seeing someone," Mia informs me as soon as Helen is out of earshot.

"Is that so? I'm glad, then, that I'm not interested in her." A sudden whoosh of cold air tingles across my skin. "Damn, it's frigid in here."

"You should feel right at home then," Mia quips. "It can't possibly be any icier than your heart."

I raise an eyebrow in question. I can't wait to hear what will spew from those kissable lips next.

"Not nice, Ms. Sousa." I step closer to her, pleased that my six-foot-six frame towers over her. I wonder if she'd be submissive to my demands between the sheets. "Let's forgo the animosity. I apologize for having said or done anything that prompted your disdain. I declare a truce."

She juts her chin out, crossing her arms over her chest. "Fine," she huffs out. "But this is my event. What I say goes. Got it?"

"Got it," I say, proffering my hand.

Her dark eyes leery, Mia places her hand in mine. "I won't let you fuck this up for me," she says, amusing me.

Chapter Eight

Mia

A dark-haired twenty-something with a cute button nose struts in my direction. She's wearing a VIP lanyard branded with a skull and crossbones around her neck, alerting me that she is a ticket holder. "Hi! I'm Rachel. Is this the dinner gathering spot?"

"Nice to meet you, Rachel. Yes, it is." I point at my lanyard, stating I'm the hostess. "I'm Mia Sousa."

"You are?" The question contains an element of surprise. "I was fortunate to cover the Hearts and Flowers event where your sister announced her retirement from modeling on my fashion blog."

Ahh ... that's why she had such a strange reaction. I should have known. Rachel must have assumed that I'd be tall and skinny like Diana. It happens all the time, and I hate it. I doubt Rachel realizes how transparent her reaction is to me. It's only natural to expect an ex-supermodel's sister to be beautiful as well. Just the same, it stings. Living in my sister's shadow can be hell. Don't get me wrong, Diana is amazing. But I don't aspire to be known for being Diana Sousa's less-than-spectacular little sister, nor do I want to be compared to her.

"OMG! I'm so stoked! I've been looking forward to this for weeks." She claps her hands together. "As a paranormal investigator, I couldn't pass up an invitation to attend the festivities taking place at Belcourt Castle."

"Awesome. I'm so happy to hear that," I say, hoping that Nathaniel doesn't catch her ear. Any disagreement between them will be detrimental. Shoving the thought aside, I watch as the ticket holders trickle from the elevator into the lobby. Several minutes pass before I excuse myself and make a beeline for the reception desk, where I've left my backpack. The hotel concierge smiles as I approach. "Looks like your event is going to be a success, Mia."

"Yay!" I giggle as I unzip the bag and pull out the clipboard containing the roster of names, along with my purple pen. "Wait until everyone sees the special surprise waiting outside the front doors. It's going to blow their minds!"

I hurry back to the gathering, introducing myself to anyone I haven't yet spoken with. Once I account for everyone, I stride to the hotel's front doors. "Please follow me. Newport's first Haunted Happenings Festival is about to begin."

Chapter Nine

Nathaniel

Cheers and applause erupt outside the hotel's main entrance. My curiosity piques as I head outside to join the others completely unprepared for the line of horse-drawn carriages awaiting us.

Chatter and laughter waft with the breeze as ticket holders clamor to find their perfect seat within one of the five ornate early 1900s-era private coaches known as Park Drags. Many vie for a spot atop the rooftop perch box, where they can converse with each other atop two facing bench seats while enjoying a crisp New England evening. Others remain inside amid the fine velvet, leather, or brocade upholstery. This lush interior comes complete with curtains and carpeted flooring.

"Well, I must commend you, Ms. Sousa." I nod toward the Park Drags. "This is beyond my expectations. You've created a memorable beginning to the festivities. I don't know how you intend to outdo this."

My heart skips a beat as she bats her long, dark eyelashes, peering up at me with an expression of glee. "Thank you, Mr.

Graves. I will take that as high praise coming from you," she says. "You should find a seat. We'll be leaving shortly."

The scent of spicy vanilla wafts around me as she moves past me, giving me ample opportunity to ogle Mia's magnificent backside as she struts away.

Too preoccupied with their excitement, no one notices that the last of the carriages remains vacant. I venture over to it, taking a seat inside while Mia converses with the driver. Her brows furrow as she appraises the coaches, pointing at mine.

"Does anyone want more legroom? Only one person sits back here." A smile that would melt even the grumpiest of hearts lights up her beautiful face as she pats the neck of a gray horse.

"This is your last chance to change seats before we leave. This spot offers comfort."

She pets the horse's nose, addresses the driver, and hops onto the footrail. "Looks like it's just you and me," she says, settling down on the seat opposite mine.

"The perfect opportunity to become better acquainted," I state.

She cocks a dark brow. "And what would you like to know? I'm an open book. Ask away."

This mode of travel is unfit for someone as tall as I am, so I stretch my long legs out before me, and the tips of my sneakers brush against the side of her boot. Since she didn't scoot out of the way like I expected, it seems like a golden opportunity to make my move. "Do you have a boyfriend?"

"Does it matter?" Too bad the startled expression thwarts her efforts to sound unfazed. Her feistiness is alluring, and once again, I ponder what it will be like to have her naked body wriggling beneath me.

"Time will tell." I run my hand over my chin, contemplating whether I should push my luck. Of course, I should. "Are you staying at the hotel?"

"Nope."

"Well, I am." I flash my most seductive smile. "You're welcome to share my room."

Crimson rises over Mia's cheeks as she sucks her bottom lip between her teeth. My dick hardens in response. Knowing I've rattled her gives me a sick satisfaction.

"That is completely inappropriate." Mia shifts beneath the heat of my gaze.

"Aw, Ms. Sousa." I move from my reclined position to lean closer to her. "It's only inappropriate if the recipient doesn't want it." Brazenly, I take her in, my eyes journeying over her from head to toe. "The rise and fall of your chest as you attempt to regain control of your racing heartbeat tells me that you want me as much as I want you."

Her lips part halfway, her breathing shallow as she stares at me. "You're a cocky son of a bitch!" Suddenly, her phone pings, and her attention moves to the message on the screen.

Fuck! I can't remember the last time I enjoyed verbal foreplay like that. It sucks that we got interrupted by a stupid text.

Clip clop ... clip clop. The horse's hooves ring out against the pavement. The carriage moves at a snail's pace, offering me a bird's-eye view of the specialty stores lining Bellevue Avenue. "I meant what I said, Ms. Sousa. This was a brilliant idea," I tell her, scowling when I note her downturned lips.

Ignoring me, Mia shakes her head while hammering out a message back. Immediately, the phone pings in response, and she tsks as she stares at the screen.

Alarm shoots through me at her visible distress. "Tell me what's going on. Maybe I can help."

"You can't." Her glassy eyes make me want to tear whoever upset her apart limb from limb. "My mother hates me. Nobody can fix that." Before the carriage slows to a complete stop, she throws the door open and jumps out.

Chapter Ten

Nathaniel

Air whooshes from my lungs, relief coursing through me. I've been holding my breath in horror as Mia careens toward the ground. Thank God she landed safely on her feet. Okay, I admit, I sound dramatic since the chances of her getting injured jumping out of a horse-drawn carriage traveling at five miles per hour max are slim. Just the same, she could have twisted her ankle or, even worse, broken a bone.

She looks up, her almond-shaped eyes locking on mine as I lean out the window, staring down at her. She reminds me of a heroine from a comic book with her olive-skinned beauty and unruly hair billowing around her shoulders. Her chest rises and falls rapidly, her ample breasts threatening to tumble from the confines of the seductive, maroon-colored lace corset. My mouth waters. Instinctively, I lick my lips, envisioning how incredible it would be to knead and suckle their lusciousness.

Her eyes widen when she notices the direction my focus has taken. She yanks the laces up, preventing any accidental spillage and denying me the pleasure of viewing her hidden treasures. Her fingers linger over the swell of each breast. My lips curve into a

Cheshire grin in knowing. I suspect we are sharing the same X-rated thoughts. Her biggest tell? The moment her breath hitches, and she sucks her plump bottom lip between her teeth.

"Mia," I say, sounding a bit more stern than necessary since she most certainly is not a child. "You scared the shit out of me. What the fuck were you thinking?"

"Don't yell at me," she says through clenched teeth. "And keep your voice down. You've nothing to worry about. I'm fine."

"I'm not yelling," I point out and then lower my voice. "And you're a terrible liar."

With a harrumph, she shoves past me and stomps toward the group of ticket holders forming at the entrance to an impressive 19th-century Gilded Age mansion. Low light flickers from the windows, casting shadows over the large expanse of the front yard. The eerie structure could rival any ghostly estate in a horror movie.

"Welcome to Belcourt Castle," Mia exclaims, extending her arm with an artistic flair toward the mansion as if she were a *Price Is Right* model, showing off a prize. She motions for us to follow her into a Renaissance-style grand foyer. A collective gasp echoes through the spacious foyer. Their heads move as if on a swivel, taking in the damask fabrics and bloodred-and-gold décor, followed by murmurs of pure awe as Mia leads them to a large circular chestnut staircase with a breathtaking stained glass bay window at the top of the landing.

"It's amazing isn't it?" Mia gushes.

"It's beyond impressive," I say after making my way to the front of the line to stand beside her. The aesthetic promises a memorable evening, which far exceeds my expectations. Surprisingly, I look forward to what is being unveiled next.

Mia smiles up at me in response. "It was love at first sight when I stepped through those doors." She points to the heavy double doors, which are now closed behind us.

Well-informed about Belcourt Castle's history, Mia regales us with accounts of its rumored haunted happenings. From an antique chest, which is reported to have erupted with smoke, to battle-worn armor known to ring out at night with screams of terror from its slain previous occupant, I find myself enraptured with the folklore. Around me, the ticket holders chatter about their own supernatural experiences. Although unlikely, many of the group claim to feel cold spots and hear strange sounds as we meander down a long hallway lit by the candles ensconced on the solid wood walls. If I weren't such a skeptic, I would be as giddy as the rest of the crowd. But as captivating as Mia's stories are, they are just fiction.

"Who's hungry?" She looks radiant, her enthusiasm contagious as the ticket holders respond with unanimous consent. Dramatically, she twirls around on one heeled lace-up boot, and then walks to the set of closed doors up ahead, throwing them open wide.

"Holy shit," I say under my breath as I follow the crowd into the dining room. A fire blazes within a gigantic fireplace, crackling and popping in perfect harmony with the French Gothic aesthetic. A massive walnut table set with sterling-silver flatware and fine porcelain dinnerware is in the middle of the room. "Everything smells delicious," I say, gazing up at the vaulted ceiling supported by steel beams.

"I hope you're hungry, Mr. Graves," Mia says.

I peer down at her, noting that the top of her head grazes my shoulders. "Famished."

With a mischievous flicker in her eye, she releases a light-hearted laugh. A melodious sound I'd sell my soul to hear for a lifetime.

Aha! I cock a brow, enjoying the game of cat and mouse. "You seem to enjoy toying with me, Ms Sousa."

She shrugs, a sly smile curving up at the corners of her lips.

I move to stand flush to her side and lean down so only she can hear me. "You know damn well what I'm starving for is a taste of you."

The hitch of her breath makes my cock twitch.

"I think I may have left a notebook up there." Mia motions to the darkened balcony overlooking the room, which she mentioned was used by orchestras during formal balls. She steps forward, surprising me when she stops to peer over her shoulder. "Care to join me?"

Chapter Eleven

Mia

I have lost my mind! My heart hammers as he follows me up the staircase. I must be. Why else would I suggest Nathaniel accompany me to the balcony, where we'll be out of sight from the ticket holders dining below?

As soon as we reach the top, Nathaniel grasps me by the hand and pulls me to him. An arm snakes around my waist, his mouth slamming down over mine, muffling my startled squeal. A deep guttural moan wrenches from his throat as his other hand moves to the base of my neck while he urges my lips to part with his tongue. Pinned against his solid strength, my breasts are flattened against him as I fist the fabric of his shirt.

"Do you enjoy teasing me?" Nathaniel asks, his hot breath scalding my cheek as he briefly breaks the kiss to gasp for breath.

"Is it working?" I ask.

He captures one of my hands, removing the splayed palm from over his pecs and down to the bulge in his pants. "What do you think?"

Possessed with unabashed desire, I barely recognize myself as my limbs grow boneless. "Touch me."

"Like this?" Nathaniel grips the fabric of my skirt, shoving it up my thigh. I suck in my breath, waiting in anticipation of what will come next. Tremors shoot through my pulsating core when his fingertip traces the exterior of my panties.

"More," I demand, desperate for Nathaniel to ease my achy need. I rise up on my tiptoes to nibble playfully at his chin.

He thrust his fingers beneath my panties, using his thumb to circle my clit. "You're soaked."

I whimper, unable to stop myself as he slides a finger into my slick pussy. In and out, fast and then slow, he finger fucks me. I throw my head back, not caring who hears us as I beg for more.

He sinks to his knees and sweeps his free arm around my back to pull my pussy to his mouth. He flashes a devilish smile and then buries his face between my thighs.

I cry out as he licks up the length of me, stopping to suck at my clit. "So sweet," he says, sliding two fingers into my throbbing center. My hips buck in response, my body surrendering to the ecstasy as he pleasures me.

"You're mine, Mia. This is just an appetizer. I'm a greedy man. Tonight, I'll feast on the main course."

My legs feel like they might give out as I rock against him. His fingers dig into the flesh of my thick thighs while he feasts on my pussy as if it were his last meal. He brings me to the breaking point, and my orgasm crashes to the surface.

Chapter Twelve

Nathaniel

"Mia? Are you up there, darling?" A woman's voice floats up from below. "All the guests are being served."

Son of a bitch! Not fucking now.

A deep, disgruntled growl lurches from my lips as I feel Mia grow rigid. Still balanced on my knees before my Gothic goddess with her ass cupped between each of my palms, I sure as fuck am not ready to leave. I'm eager for round two. My appetite for Mia's sweet pussy is not thoroughly sated.

"It's Helen," Mia whispers as if I haven't already come to that conclusion.

I move my chin to rest on the softness of Mia's tummy and peer up into her panic-filled expression. "Don't answer her. She'll go away."

Mia shakes her head, her dainty hands moving to my shoulders. "She won't."

With an exasperated sigh, I peck a kiss on her inner thigh, pissed off by the unwanted intrusion. Then I rise to my feet and cross my arms, watching as Mia smooths her skirt into place.

"Is everything okay, darling?" A woman's heels ricochet from the staircase as Helen's voice grows closer.

"I-I'm here!" Mia says, her words rushing out in a single breath. "I'll be right down. I thought I might have left one of my notebooks up here."

"There is barely any light up here," Helen says. "You should have told me before you came up alone. It's dangerous riffling around in the darkness."

"She's coming up here. Quick, hide!" With all her might, Mia pushes me toward the opposite corner. Finding her stern expression way too cute to deny, I obediently give in to her orders. Mia points at me as I stand with my back flat as a pancake against the wall. "Stay there, or else she'll see you."

I nod. "It would be terrible if she discovered my debauchery."

Mia shoots a warning glance over her shoulder as she scurries across the floor, meeting Helen just as she reaches the top of the staircase. "It's not here," Mia announces much louder than necessary. "I'd better head back down before anyone looks for me."

"Have you seen Mr. Graves?" Suspicion laces Helen's question.

"No, why?" Mia asks too quickly. "Is he missing?"

"He is," Helen says. "I'm surprised you don't know where he is since you are supposed to be his chaperone."

"Nope. No idea," Mia lies. "We should probably find out, though, before he says or does something to upset the guests."

Ouch! The reminder of our first encounter fills me with regret.

If I could turn back time, I'd erase what I said about the Haunted Happenings Festival being a farce. Not that I believe any of this paranormal nonsense is real, but because Mia is the most incredible person I've ever met. Disappearing into darkened alcoves and eating a woman out isn't my usual MO. If she'll give me the chance, I will spend every waking hour devoted to making her happy both in life and between the sheets. And should that mean I have to be amenable to Mia's belief in the afterlife, I will keep my reservations to myself. Now, I have to figure out how to convince Mia that I support her ability to succeed.

I let several moments pass before descending the staircase. Standing at the bottom, I take in the atmosphere's liveliness. Confident that everyone is too engrossed in their meals to notice me, I head out into the hallway.

I take my time, stopping to observe the many portraits that line the walls as I meander down the hallway toward the restroom. The hair on the back of my neck stands on end as an inexplicable apprehension overwhelms me. I freeze in my tracks when I see why. The blood drains from my face as my gaze lands upon a familiar set of steel-gray eyes.

What. The. Fuck?

Chapter Thirteen

Nathaniel

Mia waves me over as I reenter the dining room. Still in a daze, I stride over and lower myself onto the seat beside her.

"Where have you been?" She picks up her wineglass, her plump lips wrapping around the thin rim of the glass as she brings it to her lips. Even through my fog, I can't get the image of those same lips sucking my cock out of my mind.

"I had to go to the restroom." I pick up a linen napkin, placing it onto my lap as a server dressed in 1900s attire ladles watercress soup into my empty bowl.

After hearing Mia's accounts of Belcourt Castle's haunted history, the unexplainable coldness that has chilled my bones, and then encountering the witchy woman on the street who bore an unbelievable resemblance to the portrait hanging in the hall, I must admit I've begun to wonder whether the afterlife does exist.

"You look as white as a ghost." She giggles. "Pardon the pun."

I spoon some of the soup into my mouth. Surprisingly, it tastes better than I expected. "How do you do it?"

She looks at me with a baffled expression. "Do what?"

"Be simultaneously adorable and sexy as fuck. You're a walking temptation."

"Shhh." Her cheeks flame crimson. "Someone might hear."

"They'll be jealous if they do because I have the most delicious dessert." To prove my point, I slide my hand beneath the table and cup her mound through the fabric of her skirt. Her gasp urges me on as I lean closer. "I'm going to savor each kiss, each stroke of my finger, and every fucking thrust as you come apart begging, panting, and screaming my name."

Chapter Fourteen

Mia

Despite my best efforts, I'm too consumed with memories of my time on the balcony with Nathaniel to focus on my guests. I can't wait for the end of the event. I've lost count of the number of times I've checked the time on my cell phone. All I want is to spend the night alone with him.

Thank God, Helen announced herself before ascending the staircase. Had she walked in while my skirt was hiked up to my waist and my head tossed back in ecstasy while Nathaniel balanced on his knees worshipping my pussy, I'd have died from shame. Especially after I told Helen he was an ogre.

Nathaniel is abrupt, a tad bit cranky, and yes, there are times when he could use a filter as he sugarcoats nothing he says. But damn! Being naked and skin-on-skin with Nathaniel Graves is all I can think about.

The horse-drawn carriage ride and tonight's themed dinner were a success, and I couldn't be happier. But if we don't return to The Gilded Seashell Hotel, and I don't get into Nathaniel's bed soon, I might combust! I'm starving for more of his brand of sweet, sinful torture. Squeezing my thighs together, I watch as the ticket holders board their carriages, reminding myself that it won't be much longer before we're alone.

"Mia, darling." Helen saunters over to stand beside me. Then wraps an arm around my shoulders and hugs me to her side. "You've done a splendid job. Just as I knew you would."

I blink back the tears that threaten to spill. Receiving Helen's approval, yearning to be beneath Nathaniel's powerful body, and praying all week that people receive Haunted Happenings well are making me a fucking wreck. All the nervousness, wanting, and thankfulness bubble up inside me as I struggle to remain grounded. "Thank you. Hopefully, everyone will enjoy tomorrow's events just as much."

"They will," a familiar masculine voice assures us. I peer over my shoulder, my stomach doing somersaults as Nathaniel steps out from the carriage house. His long-legged strides exude confidence as he slips his cell phone into the pocket of his unzipped leather jacket. Filled with sheer lust, I wish I could run my hands over the body-hugging T-shirt he wears underneath.

Helen's keen gaze moves from me to Nathaniel before lowering down just in time to catch his pinky finger entwining with mine.

"Mr. Graves." Helen nods.

"Ms. Carrington." Nathaniel's lips curve up into a devilish smile that have me questioning if Dracula himself might be one of his relatives.

"I'm sure you agree Mia deserves tremendous praise for such a delightful evening," Helen says. "I'm sure it will be enjoyable for you to relay the details of tonight's event with your readers."

"Well, not *all* the details," Nathaniel replies, ignoring my sharp intake of breath.

Helen cocks an eyebrow at me, her expression knowing. "Yes, you're correct, Mr. Graves. You wouldn't want to divulge every-thing in your column. Next year's guests will be anxious to uncover *tricks* and *treats* of their own."

"Oh..." I clap my hands together, interrupting them. "It looks like everyone has taken their places. We're holding up progress."

"Go on." Helen winks. "Have fun."

Chapter Fifteen

Mia

Satisfied that everyone is aboard their carriages, I confirm with the driver that it's time to leave—finally! Adrenaline flows within me as I bound down to the last carriage. I take Nathaniel in. Seated with his hands clasped on his lap and his long, muscular legs outstretched with his ankles crossed, Nathaniel's raw masculinity nearly takes my breath away.

"Let me help," he says, reaching out for me as I hike up my skirt and step up onto the running board.

"It's alright. I've got this." What I lack in height, I make up for with curvaceous hips, a big booty, and a pair of double Ds. If Nathaniel were to injure himself hefting me up onto the carriage, it would be too much of a reminder of Mother telling me I need to lose weight.

"I insist," he says, his large hand enveloping mine and then plucking me up as if I were a lightweight. I yelp in surprise as his hands move to my hips, maneuvering me backward to flop down onto his lap.

"This is where you belong. Seated right here," he whispers against my ear. With a contented sigh, I close my eyes, enjoying the sensation of his hand fondling my breast. I recline against him as his other hand slips lower to smooth over the top of my thigh.

"We shouldn't be doing this here." My halfhearted protest goes unnoticed as a whimper oozes from my lips, my head lolling back as his hand plunges beneath my bodice.

"Tell me you don't want me to play with you, and I'll stop," Nathaniel says, distracting me from reason as he rolls a puckered nipple between his thumb and forefinger. He bucks his hips up, grinding his erection against my swollen folds. "Do you know how hard it is not to pull off your panties so you can ride my cock right now?"

My hips roll of their own accord, bearing down on his hardness. Exhilaration heightens the moment as we dry-hump, heedless of the other carriages' occupants only a few feet ahead.

"You're a fucking dream," Nathaniel grits out between clenched teeth. "So eager for my cock. But not yet. A quickie won't be enough to sate my appetite. I plan to take my time. Taste and drink your juices and make you cum over and over again until you can't remember your own name."

Chapter Sixteen

Mia

Forty-five minutes later, I step into Nathaniel's hotel room and stare impatiently at his broad back as he hangs the do not disturb sign on the doorknob. Finally, the deadbolt clicks, and he moves toward me. I watch with bated breath, my heart fluttering as his fingers move to the buttons of his shirt, unbuttoning them as he prowls toward me with the ease of a panther stalking its prey. "It's about time I've got you all to myself."

Butterflies swarm in my stomach as the back of his hand brushes over my cheek. "Mia Sousa, you're bewitching," he says as he cups my face between his open palms. He looms above me, his head lowering to feather light kisses along my forehead, then atop my nose. He pauses when he reaches my mouth. His lips linger over mine, his breath hot as the tip of his tongue flicks out before his mouth crashes to mine. The gentleness of his kisses erupts into a shared passion-fueled frenzy. He moves his hand to the base of my neck, his kiss deepening while his other hand journeys lower, smoothing over the side of my breasts to caress my hip.

I flatten my palms against the wall, searching for the light switch, and gasp when his fingers clamp over my wrist, halting my progress. "What the hell do you think you're doing?" Dark eyes bore into mine as he glares down at me.

"I was going to get undressed. So I thought I should turn off the light."

He gaps at me with a look of disbelief. "No fucking way." His fingers close over mine, stopping me from turning the switch. "There is no way in hell you're going to deny me the pleasure of admiring your naked body." His head moves lower, his stubbled cheek scratching mine as he nibbles the tender skin behind my ear. "I've been lusting after those tits all night?" His mouth journeys lower, brushing kisses along the swell of my breasts. Before I know what's happening, my corset is on the floor, my bra lying in a heap on top of it.

"Fuck ... your tits are amazing." The tip of his tongue flicks out over his lips. I've never seen desire that intense directed at me. Electricity courses through me as my body trembles with need. "Come," he says, taking my hand in his and guiding me farther into the room. "Get on the bed, and brace yourself on all fours, your head facing me."

I crawl onto it and position myself as he commanded.

"Good girl." He lowers the zipper of his pants and pushes them down to the floor along with his white boxer shorts.

I suck my lip between my teeth, taking in his thick, long cock. He fists it, stroking up and down as he moves closer to bring it to my mouth. He rubs the engorged head over my lips, coating them with precum. "Umm," I groan, licking the saltiness with my tongue. "More," I demand, opening my mouth.

"As you wish," he says, thrusting his dick between my lips and not stopping until it hits the back of my throat.

My cheeks hollow as I suck like a woman starved. I moan with pleasure as his hips buck, his balls hitting my chin as I take all of him to the back of my throat.

"That's my girl," he says through gritted teeth. His head arches back, the veins of his neck bulging as I grip his cock with one hand and pump. Faster and faster, I work his cock, my eyes watering as he grows rigid, his body spasming moments before he climaxes into my mouth.

Chapter Seventeen

Nathaniel

The way she looks with her swollen red lips still wrapped around my cock, milking the last of my cum, is the most beautiful sight I've ever seen. A small, disgruntled sound escapes her lips as I step backward to withdraw my cock. "Aw ... my beautiful Gothic goddess has yet to be satisfied. Your pussy is aching for me to fill it up, isn't it?"

Mia hasn't moved, her arms shaking as she balances on all fours. Does she grasp what she means to me? How her curly dark purple-streaked hair cascading in a tousled mess over her shoulders, her eyes glazed over with lust, and the perspiration glistening on her skin turn me on?

"Do you know how gorgeous you look with those tits hanging heavy and free? How they make my dick hard and my hands itch to play with them."

"Why don't you?" A shit-eating grin crosses her lips. "What are you waiting for?"

No need to ask me twice. I bound forward, my hands plunging to cup her breasts. "Your tits were made to be held in my big hands." Mia's murmurs of need ignite a fire in me. I play with her breasts, testing their weight in my palms, and then roll the puckered tips between my thumbs and forefingers. "Take the rest of your clothes off. Then lie on your back at the edge of the bed with your legs spread wide."

Face flushed, Mia rises from the bed. She reaches behind her to unzip her skirt and then slips it down over her womanly curves and onto the floor.

"Panties, too," I say as she pauses in hesitation. "Do it. Now. I need to see your pretty little pussy."

Clad only in red satin panties, she sucks in her lower lip between her teeth, her fingers stalling when they reach the waistband.

"You've got exactly two seconds to take those damn things off before I do it for you." Part of me wishes she wouldn't obey. Then I could teach her a lesson. Her round ass would look so pretty while I spank it pink.

Her breasts heave as she inhales and then slides the panties down to the floor. Nude, she saunters to the bed. As she's been instructed, she sits down on its edge, then reclines onto her back, allowing her shapely legs to hang over the edge. My cock pulses as her thick thighs spread wide, revealing her slickness.

"Such a good girl," I say, lowering onto my knees. Gripping each of her ankles, I place them over my shoulders, then bury my head between her warm, satiny thighs. Flattening my tongue, I lick up her center and stop to suckle her clit, savoring her taste as I inhale her intoxicating womanly fragrance and delight in the taste of her salty juices coating my tongue.

"Oh. My. God," Mia says. Her head lolls right and left, and her eyes roll back as if possessed when I insert a finger into her tightness. She fists the hair at the base of my neck, her groans growing louder. "Don't stop. Please," she begs. "Don't stop."

"No fucking way." My cock throbs with the want to fill her as her creamy juices drip down my arm. "I want you soaked when I slip inside this beautiful, tight cunt."

Her hips buck up, her torso arching off the mattress. Greedily, I latch onto her clit, licking and sucking and feeding my craving for her. A sharp cry ricochets off the walls around us as I thrust a second finger inside her and a third at the entrance of her taboo hole.

"Nathaniel!" Mia screams, her nails digging into my shoulders as she shatters around me, her climax coming long and hard.

I massage her thighs, my palms running up and down their length as I blow against her pussy as she shakes with aftershocks. Once the aftershocks subside and I'm certain she's ready for more, I lie down at the top of the bed.

"Mia, we're not done yet." I pat the pillow next to mine. "Come here."

If this were the last day of my life, I'd die a happy man. A feeling of contentment overwhelms me as she rejects the pillow, choosing to rest her head on my shoulder instead. The sense of peace I thought lost forever after my parents' death washes through me. Could this be love? I've never felt so protective of a woman before. It seems inconceivable, considering we've just met. But maybe that witchy woman really cast a spell. My heart tells me Mia is the woman who will eventually become my wife, the mother of my unborn children—my life.

I lift up onto my shoulder to look down at her. Gently, I lift her chin with my thumb to gaze into her lovely eyes. I lower my mouth to brush her lips with mine, enjoying the taste of my saltiness on her tongue.

Mia rolls onto her back and then wraps her legs around my hips. "This is going to change everything," I say as I position my cock at her entrance

"I know," Mia says.

I ease into her warmth, relishing the tightness. "You okay?" I ask, shaking with need for her as I wait for her confirmation before I claim her as mine forever.

"I want this. I want you to be my first," Mia says. The trust in her dark eyes melts my heart. "Please, Nathaniel. Make love to me."

Possessiveness surges within me as I push through the barrier. I stare down at her, hating myself for the grimace of pain that crosses her face as she clamps her eyes shut. "Look at me," I say, rocking my hips slowly to give her time to adjust to my size. Her eyes flutter open, and I'm relieved to see they've darkened into a haze of pleasure.

She moans as I start to move faster. It doesn't take long for Mia to match my pace. Before I know it, I'm pounding into her, my breathing labored as she screams her release moments before my cum spurts into her, filling her with my seed.

Chapter Eighteen

Nathaniel

The woman has me bewitched. She's a fucking sorceress. I stand beneath the showerhead, the warm water easing the stiffness from my shoulders. I wish Mia were here with me. We stayed wrapped up in each other's arms much later than planned this morning. As much as I hated to see her leave, I understood that if she stayed any longer, she'd never be ready in time to welcome everyone for breakfast. There will be plenty of time for showers together in the future when she isn't obligated with her Haunted Happening duties.

I rub the bar of soap between my palms. Once a thick lather forms, I fist my cock, desperate to ease the aching need. All the while, I envision Mia, looking so damn pretty, on her knees, her plump ruby-red lips wrapped around my dick as she sucks me to oblivion.

I'm half tempted to head to her room, pound on the door, and have my way with her when she answers. Fuck those Haunted Happening goers. They can wait, for all I care. But Mia cares about them, and because she does, so do I.

With teeth clenched, I tighten my grip, pumping harder. A guttural growl rolls from my chest as my breathing labors. Seconds later, my body quakes, and cum spurts in rivers down my hand and arm. I rest my head on the tile as I come back down to earth. Just the thought of Mia drives me mad. I've never cum so hard in my life.

After a thorough cleansing, I step out of the shower and note the vibration of my cell on the counter. Hope soars within me. Could it be Mia saying she misses me too? Water drips onto the floor as I reach the phone in two long strides. Reality slaps me in the face as I read the name on the caller ID and swipe to accept the call. "Nathaniel Graves speaking," I answer instinctively, going into professional mode.

"Good morning, Mr. Graves. This is Andrea from *Global Destinations Magazine*. I'm Charles Hastings's personal assistant. If you have a few moments, Mr. Hastings would like to speak with you."

"Right now?" I realize that my response makes me sound like an idiot. Everyone knows that the news doesn't stop just because it's Saturday. In my field, work assignments fill the weekends.

Get a grip, Graves.

I reach for a towel and wrap it around my waist. Then I pad back into the bedroom area. I can't allow my personal feelings toward Mia to cloud my judgment. I clear my throat, doing my best not to think about her warm, curvaceous body beneath mine or the heart-melting smile she lavished on me as I slid inside her sweet pussy. I sit down on the edge of the rumpled bed, hardly cold from our night of bliss.

"Andrea, please pardon my reaction. A knock on the door had distracted me when I picked up your call," I say. "Of course, I have time to speak with Mr. Hastings."

"Oh, no worries, Mr. Graves," Andrea says. "I hope you enjoy the rest of your day. I'll get Mr. Hastings now. Please hold."

The phone clicks, followed by some horrible-sounding techno music. Silence would have been preferable. If I'm offered the job, what the hell am I going to do? Until twenty-four hours ago, the answer was a no-brainer. Overnight, my life got complicated. Can I pack up and leave for New York City without seeing how things work out with Mia?

Chapter Nineteen

Mia

"Everything looks amazing." My sister, Diana, surveys her surroundings, ignoring the whispers and stares directed at her while her husband, Javier, steps forward and back to trigger the motion detector of an animated life-sized witch, making her cackle.

Diana, Katie, and I spent part of our Thursday afternoon carving various shapes and sizes of pumpkins. Then we headed over to Bon Appétit, the restaurant located inside The Gilded Seashell Hotel, to create a kick-ass Halloween display at the entrance. Using the witch as our focal point, we embellished her traditional black attire with a crow resting on her shoulder and a decorative broom in her hand. Around her, we arranged haystacks of varying heights. Atop each haystack, we placed one or more jack-o'-lanterns, each illuminated by a flameless candle inside. To tie it all together, we hid a smoke machine within the display that wafted purple smoke high into the air. The hotel manager agreed to stream the Halloween Spotify playlist I'd created during breakfast. The music adds the perfect touch to the spooky ambiance.

"He's such a dork." I shake my head in amusement at Javier's shenanigans. Adoration shines in Diana's eyes as she watches her husband make a complete ass of himself. "But I love him, anyway. He's an awesome brother-in-law."

"There's Katie," Javier exclaims, waving her over to the display. My usually reserved friend has joined Javier, and together, they wiggle their hands and feet, roaring with laughter.

"Oh boy, Javier has found a partner in crime." Diana laughs softly before taking on a more somber tone. "I spoke with Mother before leaving the house." Diana pats my arm as she always does before she relays something she feels might hurt my feelings. I'm surprised I still have skin, considering the number of times she's felt the need to do so. "Mother wanted me to tell you she woke up with a migraine and would do her best to attend the masquerade ball tonight. However, it will depend on how she feels."

"You and I both know that's an excuse. She won't come." Although I'm not surprised and should be used to it by now, the slight still stings. Mother always comes up with some sorry-ass reason she can't partake in anything that has to do with me. "Don't give me that look."

"I'm not giving you any look," Diana says.

"Yes, you are. It's the same expression you have each time you must do Mother's dirty work." I head over to a nearby table, pointing at the small potted mum placed in the middle. "This was a great idea," I say, complimenting my sister's suggestion for the centerpieces.

"Thank you," Diana says, a note of disdain in her tone. "It's Mother's loss. If she truly has a headache, she needs to take flipping headache medicine and deal with it. This is your big moment. What you've accomplished is terrific. Promise me that you won't let her ignorance put a damper on any of this."

"I won't," I say, quickly changing the subject. "You might want to tear your husband away from the display. He and Katie are causing a ruckus." A small group gathered around it, all acting like children. "Tell him the witch is his at the end of the ball."

"I'll let you tell him yourself." Diana entwines her arm with mine, and together, we set out to break up the chaos.

"The breakfast buffet is ready. "I hope everyone is hungry for some ghost waffles and egg eyes."

"Ghost waffles!" Javier and Katie declare in unison.

"Mm-hmm." I laugh. "It's a themed breakfast with all kinds of tricks and treats. The kitchen staff even created pumpkin-shaped pancakes with chocolate chip eyes!"

Tingles prick my skin, and unease floods me from out of nowhere. I move my attention to the lobby, surprised to see Nathaniel conversing with the concierge. "You should get your food while it's hot. I'll be right in."

As I stride through the lobby, my gut instinct tells me I won't be happy when I find out what's going on. "Everything all right?" I ask, wondering why Nathaniel has pursed his lips.

"It's just work. I'll tell you about it later." Nathaniel places his hand on my lower back, leading me back toward the restaurant. "I'm famished. How about you?"

"Starving," I say. "I worked up an appetite last night."

We fill our plates to overflowing with anything and everything pumpkin spice, then join Diana, Javier, and Katie at their table. Rachel makes an uninvited visit to the table to gush over my sister. Meanwhile, Nathaniel remains mute. No playful behavior and colorful innuendos as he'd done the previous night. No forbidden touches beneath the table or efforts to lure me into a secret spot for stolen kisses.

Something is amiss. I just hope nothing I've done has triggered his strange mood. After last night, I assumed he'd be more forthcoming with his emotions. Shoving my anxieties aside, I stand with my juice glass held high. Tapping it with a fork, I announce the Haunted Happenings Public Street Fair will open in fifteen minutes.

Immediately, the ticket holders abandon their tables and head outside. Diana and Javier are excited to attend a seminar on the holistic use of herbs, while Katie is looking forward to purchasing a new crystal to add to her growing collection.

"Your sister and her husband are very nice. Katie, too," Nathaniel says once we're alone.

"They are." Pride wells within me. "I'm pretty fond of them myself."

His lips quirk into a half-smile. "I'm surprised your parents didn't come."

"Don't be," I say. "My mother doesn't really like me. She puts up with me."

He shoots a look of disbelief my way. "How could anyone not like you?" His stern expression softens. "You're irresistible."

I shrug, uncertain how much of my dysfunctional relationship with my mother I should confide in Nathaniel. "Mother always accused me of navigating through life with an artistic flair." I squish my nose up, my mouth twisting back and forth as I contemplate what to say next. "She told me with my theatrics I could give any motion picture actress a run for their money, but since I wasn't pretty enough, or thin enough, or smart enough..."

"What the fuck?" Nathaniel gulps the rest of his orange juice and, with more force than necessary, slams the glass back down onto the table. "Is she visually impaired? If not, it's obvious she's incredibly stupid."

Nathaniel's vehement response is unexpected. I release a long-drawn-out breath, finding it difficult to go on. "She thinks I'm a disappointment. Nothing I do is ever enough." I swipe a tear from the corner of my eye. It's embarrassing to admit my mother cast me aside, but I'm more concerned that Nathaniel might decide he's been mistaken about his feelings for me. I don't think I could handle the rejection if he thought Mother was right and tossed me aside too.

Nathaniel grips each of my shoulders using his strong hands to maneuver me in my chair to face him. "Listen." His chin flexes as he tips my chin up to meet his eyes. "You're an enigma, Ms. Sousa." His free hand slides behind my shoulders stopping to cup the nape of my neck. "You fascinate me." His lips lower to my mouth. Both passionate and tender, I collapse into Nathaniel's arms and allow him to kiss away my insecurities.

Chapter Twenty

Nathaniel

Overnight, Belcourt Castle's expansive grounds have transformed into a carnival-like atmosphere. Colorful tents bustle with activity while the sweet and savory scents from the food trucks waft through the air.

"Let's have our fortunes told," Mia suggests as we walk hand in hand among the crowd.

"Don't tell me you're serious. You're too smart to spend your money on a load of crap."

"Is not." Mia steers me toward Madame Tejada's ticket booth. "Have you ever gone to a fortune teller before?"

"No." I roll my eyes to the heavens. "It's bull shit."

"Then how do you know it's a load of bull if you haven't been to one before?" Jaw set, Mia reminds me of a petulant child as she squints up at me.

"Because I just do," I answer.

Her long braid whips left and right as she shakes her head. "That is not an appropriate answer. You are being rather closed-minded, don't you think?"

"Nope," I say, and then, knowing I'll get a rise out of her, I can't resist stooping to whisper in her ear, "I should fist that braid between my fingers as I bend you over my knees and spank that delectable ass for challenging me."

Her gasp makes my cock twitch, and I wish like hell I didn't have to leave for New York in a few hours. After confiding in me this morning, she was too vulnerable. I know it will be difficult to convince her that long-distance relationships are hard, but with effort, they could work. I just hope she'll forgive me for leaving before the ball tonight.

"Alright," I say. If sitting with a fortune teller will make her happy, then I'll do it. "I'm game. Let's get the tickets."

"Yay!" Mia jumps up and down, shrieking with excitement. "You won't regret it."

Before I have time to change my mind, I purchase two admissions. As we turn away from the ticket booth, an attendant holds the tent flap open, motioning for us to enter the dark, candlelit area. Although it's difficult to make out her facial features, something about Madame Tejada seems familiar.

"Come in. Don't be shy," she coaxes. "I've been expecting you."

"Really?" Mia skips to the table and sits down while I remain rooted in place.

Mia looks over her shoulder, pulling on the back of the chair beside her. "Don't be a chicken. Sit down."

I waver briefly and then lower onto the seat beside Mia. The air feels heavy, and Madame Tejada's eerie familiarity creeps me out.

The fortune teller places the deck of tarot cards before me. "Shuffle the cards, dear one."

Dear One.

Instantly, I stiffen at the use of the endearment. The witchy woman called me that too. My fingers shake as I shuffle the deck while Madame Tejada explains that by having me do so, I'll infuse the cards with my energy.

"That should be sufficient," Madame Tejeda says. "Now draw one and give me the rest. Hmm..." Madame Tejada assesses the card for several moments before she speaks. "You've experienced trauma at an early age. It's no wonder you're so skeptical about believing in the unseen."

She's hit too close to home. I shift, uncomfortable with anything related to my upbringing. Mia leans forward, engrossed in the reading while Madame Tejada continues. "Your family is always with you, Nathaniel."

"How do you know my name?" I question, unable to disguise the leeriness in my tone. "You never asked for it."

Madame Tejada chortles. "I'm a fortune teller," she states matter-of-factly. "I know everything. Including the car accident. And I know you can't bring yourself to believe that ghosts exist because that would force you to confront your past."

"Enough!" I bolt upright, and my chair crashes backward onto the floor. "Mia," I bellow. "Time to go."

Chapter Twenty-One

Nathaniel

I burst through the opening of the tent with Mia in hot pursuit. My stomach roils, and I fall to my knees. spewing the contents of my breakfast into the manicured bushes that form a barrier between Belcourt Castle and the other residents along the street. My shoulders shudder with dry heaves, my skin clammy with perspiration as I rock forward with my head hanging low. Mia's concern is understandable as she kneels by my side. "Talk to me, Nate. Tell me what's wrong. You've seemed off since breakfast."

"How did they know?" I question wide-eyed as I pant for breath.

"They?" Mia asks. "Who are you talking about?"

"The sins of my past are being dredged up by strangers who shouldn't know a damn thing about me." Peering up into Mia's worry-filled gaze, I know I sound delusional.

"It's okay, Nate." Mia puts her hand on my shoulder to comfort me. "You can tell me anything."

Eyes closed, I prayed to a God who abandoned me years ago to help me explain everything to Mia. To help me be free of the hellish battle I've lived with for all these years. But what if I tell her about my past, and she decides I'm a monster? Somehow, if she doesn't, when I tell her about the new job, she'll definitely want nothing more to do with me.

"Nothing you could tell me will change my feelings for you because even though we just met, I've fallen hard." Mia's voice softens. "I know it's soon, but I've fallen in love with you."

"Mia," I say her name with the reverence of a prayer. "You're a dream. My sweet angel by day and my Gothic goddess by night. Why love a jaded man like me when you could do so much better?"

Chapter Twenty-Two

Mia

Neither of us speaks as we make our way through the lobby of the Gilded Seashell Hotel, we don't stop to converse with anyone. Instead, we head straight for the elevators. Enclosed in the small space, I wish for him to say something—anything. But he doesn't. Not even when he opens his hotel room's door and gestures for me to go in.

I comply when he motions for me to sit down on the bed and watch as he closes the curtains. Then returns to where I'm seated and kneels before me. Wordlessly, he positions each of my legs around his waist. Then startles me as he locks his arms around my back and rests his head against my breast. I fork my fingers through his thick brown hair to comfort him as he squeezes me tight. Vulnerability shows in his dark, soulful eyes as he stares up at me. "Please don't hate me."

"Never. I love you too much." I smooth my hand over his broad back while he clings to me, searching for the right words to convey my love.

"I was just a kid. I didn't mean any harm." His voice quakes, his body trembling as he reveals the details of his past. "I killed them. My family is dead, and it's because of me."

"Nate," I sniffle, wishing I could take away his anguish.

"I was sixteen. I'd just gotten my driver's license. My parents had taken my sister and me out for dinner to celebrate. Then my father handed me the keys to drive home. Like an idiot, I showed off. Dad told me to slow down, but I took the corner too fast and lost control of the vehicle." He pauses on a sharp intake of breath, and his shoulders shake as tears stream down his face. "I woke up with tubes in my nose, a broken arm and leg, and a collapsed lung the following day. But I was still breathing."

My sweatshirt is wet from his tears. "Shhh," I say, trying my best to console Nathaniel.

"When the police came into my hospital room to question me, they were the ones who told me I was the sole survivor."

His grief feels like a knife in the heart. If only I could take away his pain. "It was an accident, my love. A horrible accident."

"I prayed they would visit me in a dream to tell me they were happy and in a better place." His eyes are wide as he looks up to shake his head. "It never happened."

"Oh, Nate," I say, rocking him against me as he squeezes me tighter. "You did nothing different from any other sixteen-year-old with car keys. It's obvious your family loved you. I'm certain they wouldn't want you to suffer from guilt. Please stop torturing yourself."

It feels like an eternity passes before his breathing steadies. "I accepted the position with the *Global Destinations.*"

"That's fantastic," I say, not expecting him to transition into a work discussion after pouring his heart out.

He pushes away from me. Then he moves to sit down beside me on the edge of the bed and takes my hands in his. "It's not."

"It isn't?" I attribute his grim expression to his breakdown, not the bombshell he drops on me next. "I'm sorry, Mia." He rubs his

66

red-rimmed eyes. "The position is in the New York office. I must leave for the city before the ball starts. My first assignment requires me to be on a plane to Ireland tomorrow at 5:30 a.m."

Chapter Twenty-Three

Mia

My eyes burn as I stand on the balcony overlooking the courtyard below. I needed a breather away from everyone to gather my thoughts. Alone except for the crickets who serenade me, I attempt to comprehend the incomprehensible.

The feelings I have for Nathaniel were the last thing I'd expected when I'd walked into the headquarters of *Paradise and Pleasure Magazine*. Especially after my disdain for his arrogant demeanor, and the worry I had about him possibly ruining Haunted Happenings.

Now, after placing a check mark on the calendar each night before bed as I counted down the days to the Haunted Happenings Festival and spending every spare moment during the waking hours of the day planning its activities, I've earned the right to bask in its success. Yet nothing could have prepared me for this all-encompassing sorrow eating away at my soul.

"Why are you hiding out here, darling? You should be inside celebrating." Helen's throaty voice comes from behind me, followed by the familiar *click-clop* of her stiletto heels.

"I don't want to jinx it," I lie.

"With over a thousand email inquiries received this afternoon questioning when, where, and how to get tickets for next year's event?" Helen asks in disbelief. "Haunted Happenings is one hundred percent going to become an annual event. I've already spoken with my secretary, and she has selected several dates that she believes will work for next year. I told her you'd call her on Monday to review them."

I force a halfhearted smile. "Okay. I'll check in after class."

"It's just spectacular how the moon shines tonight. You can't get a more picturesque aesthetic than that," Helen says.

"It's pretty perfect—the full moon I mean," I say absently.

"He'll be back." Helen's comment brings me back to the present. Her keen eyes and knowing smile bewilder me as I turn to face her.

"How did you find out?" I ask.

"That Nathaniel Graves has stolen your heart?" Helen asks, waiting for me to nod before she continues. "It's written all over your face just as it's written in the stars."

"But he left. I watched him drive away." I sniffle, swallowing back the hurt. "If he cared, why would he have done that?"

"Because men, my dear one, are daft sometimes." She playfully nudges me with her shoulder. "In case you are unaware, you own his heart as well."

"He said he wanted to continue our relationship," I tell her, contemplating whether our love will be strong enough to survive the distance.

"Oh, darling. Sometimes we must risk losing what we value most before we come to our senses. Fate has a way of finding us when we least expect it. Its timing is never convenient." She lowers her voice into a hushed whisper. "Want to know a secret?"

"A secret?" Nothing thrills me more than learning something nobody else knows.

"You promise not to tell a soul?" Helen questions.

I made the sign of the cross over my heart.

"Not even Katie?" Amusement flickers in her eyes.

"Mm-hmm," I say with a vigorous nod. "Not even Katie."

"Researchers can trace my great-great-great-grandmother back to the Salem witch trials. Her name was Elizabeth. There is a portrait of her in the hallway if you would like to see what she looks like. Before they burned her at the stake, she shared her knowledge of spells and mystical things with her daughter. Ever since, the gift has been passed down to each generation's female children. Although I have no daughters of my own, I continue to share my knowledge with others as Madame Tejada."

My mouth falls. "You're Madame Tejada?"

"Shhh, not so loud." Helen looks wearily around. "He might hear you."

From the corner of my eye, I glimpse a man's dark suit. His presence draws my attention toward the doors as my stomach somersaults.

Turning around with a wink, Helen walks toward the drop-dead gorgeous hunk of a man. "It's about time you arrived. It's rude to leave a beautiful young woman without a dance partner at the ball," she says before disappearing into the crowded ballroom.

"Nate, what are you doing here? You're supposed to be in New York," I say, clutching the railing to keep from fainting.

"I told Charles Hastings I'd changed my mind, and although I appreciated the opportunity, the woman I love lives in Rhode Island. They didn't like that, but understood my future is with you."

The relief I feel from Nathaniel's admission is beyond words. "I swear I will do everything in my power to never make you regret that decision."

I shiver as his fingertip moves to graze over the swell of my breasts. His smile is suggestive, and his eyes flicker with raw lust. "You look breathtaking. Ball gowns suit you."

"I'll fill my closet with them, and I'll wear a new one just for you every single day." The promise comes out in a single, rushed breath, my heart thrumming and pulse racing.

"I will enjoy stripping it from your gorgeous body," he says, his voice having grown huskier. He tilts my chin with his thumb and forefinger, his other hand sweeping around my back. I gasp as he pulls me flush against his chest and slams his mouth to mine. As if starved, he nibbles the corner of my lip before plunging his tongue inside.

A guttural protest is wrenched from his lips as I break the kiss. "I need to find Katie," I say breathlessly.

"Where did that thought come from?" He chuckles. "You wound me. Especially after that kiss."

"I need Katie to cover for me because I'm going to die if you don't fuck me. She can tell everyone I was sick and had to leave early."

"I like how you think." Amusement laces Nathaniel's words. "Let's go find her. But we can't leave yet."

"You're right." I sigh. "It wouldn't look good to leave my event before it ends." Arm in arm, we stroll back into the ballroom. Before I went outside, Katie was standing by the bar with her date. Now, I don't see either of them anywhere. Unease creeps through me. "I don't know where she is."

Nathaniel selects a scallop wrapped in bacon from a silver tray held out to him by one of the catering staff. "Do you think she left?" he asks, popping it into his mouth.

"It isn't like her to leave without telling me, but I know she was uncomfortable with the revealing ball gown her boyfriend, Padrig, guilted her into buying. She could have gone home to change."

"Why would she have given in to wearing something she didn't like?" Nathaniel asks.

"Because she doesn't always have a backbone. She's too nice and always wants to make everyone happy, even at her own expense." Suddenly, I spot Padrig by the side entrance. "There he is. Let's go ask him."

Sure enough, Padrig confirms Katie has indeed headed home. However, something in his tone doesn't sit right with me. He seems preoccupied and uninterested in speaking with us. It almost feels as if he's hiding something.

Just after midnight, the last of the guests finally depart. "The two of you don't need to stay with me. I'll lock up," Helen says, assuring us it's fine to leave when we gave a halfhearted protest. "I'm not afraid of any ghosts who haunt this home. After all, they are all my ancestors."

When we reach the wrought-iron gate, Nathaniel turns around to take a final look at Belcourt Castle. "Who is that woman looking out the window with Helen?"

"I don't see anyone except Helen." I shrug. "Maybe it's a shadow."

"Perhaps," Nathaniel says, taking my hand. He smiles down at me with undisguised affection. "You saved me from myself. If not for you, I wouldn't have accepted my past and given in to the magical beauty of the unknown. Thanks for bringing me back to life. I love you today, tomorrow, and forever."

Learn about Diana and Javier's unlikely romance in Kissed by Desire.
Read here: https://a.co/d/6qkV4oK

Dear Reader,

Thank you so much for picking up *Haunted by Desire*! I hope you fell in love with Mia and Nathaniel's story as much as I loved writing it. These two completely stole my heart, and bringing their romance to life was such a joy.

If you've never visited Newport or stepped inside the hauntingly beautiful Belcourt Castle, I hope you'll add it to your bucket list. With its rich history of ghostly whispers and even its modern-day brush with fame (yes, Jennifer Lawrence celebrated her wedding there!), it felt like the perfect backdrop for Mia's Haunted Happenings Festival.

I'd be so grateful if you could leave a quick, honest review on Amazon, Goodreads, or BookBub. Reviews not only help other readers discover *Haunted by Desire* but also make a huge difference in spreading the love for this story.

Amazon	Goodreads	BookBub

Thank you again for being such an important part of this journey. Your support means the world.

XOXO,
Valerie

The Seaside Desire World

**Interconnected standalone romances
located in Newport, Rhode Island.**

The Literary Ladies Duet: Full-length Novels

The Prodigal's Desire, The Literary Ladies #1
https://books2read.com/u/bOxYJA
Forever His Desire, The Literary Ladies #2
https://books2read.com/u/mZrQJR

**The Literary Ladies
A Seaside Desire Special Edition Box Set**
https://books2read.com/u/3kPVrK

Seasons of Love:
Short Contemporary Romance (1-2 hour reads)

Kissed by Desire, Seasons of Love #1
https://books2read.com/u/baVx82
Haunted by Desire, Seasons of Love #2
https://books2read.com/u/4Ae1ye

**Coming Soon
The O'Hallorans:**
Short Contemporary Romance (1-2 hour reads)
A Date with Desire, The O'Hallorans #1
Ms. Carrington's Desire, The O'Hallorans #2
Danger, Deceit, and Desire, The O'Hallorans #3

About the Author

Valerie Lynne is a self-confessed word junkie in love with romance. By day she works in financial services, and by night she writes small town contemporary romance that sizzles. Valerie has a passion for coffee, chihuahuas, fashion illustration, and anything girly or pink. She spends her free time collecting dolls, amassing more books for her ever-growing TBR pile, watching baseball or game shows, and hanging out with friends and family. A lifetime Rhode Islander, she lives with two very spoiled chihuahuas, Chanel and Gianni.

Follow Valerie on social. She's always happy to connect with fellow book lovers.

www.ingramcontent.com/pod-product-compliance
Lightning Source LLC
Chambersburg PA
CBHW071236170626
46809CB00008BA/3082